Doggie Doesn't Know "No!"

Written by Cindy R. Lee
Illustrated by Kent Hathaway

Cindy R. Lee, LCSW, LADC
PO Box 14060
Oklahoma City, OK 73113

The "Accepting No" concept as it relates to "children from hard places" was derived from the Trust-Based Relational Intervention ® resources (Purvis & Cross, 1999-2014.) For more information, please read Purvis, K.B., Cross, D.R. & Sunshine, W.L. (2007) *The Connected Child: Bringing Hope and Healing to Your Adoptive Family.* New York: McGraw- Hill.

Acknowledgements:
Thank you to Christopher, Amanda and Jack for all their advice, input and support. Special thanks to Kelly and Amy Gray, David and Jean McLaughlin and the McLaughlin Family Foundation for giving the gift of healing to foster and adopted children. Thank you to Casey Call, Henry Milton, Brooke Hayes and Jennifer Abney for all their support and guidance. Gratitude also goes to Cheryl Devoe for donating her time and editing skills to this project.

Special thanks to the Central Oklahoma Humane Society for all their hard work and dedication in finding forever homes for Oklahoma's four-legged friends. Thank you to Rufus, the comfort dog, for visiting HALO Project foster children.

Dedicated to David, Jean, Kelly, Amy
Lainey, Katherine, Georgia, Geno & Annie

Thank you for all you do for
children from hard places.

Accepting No – Teaching Tips for Parents

By Cindy R. Lee, LCSW, LADC

Doggie Doesn't Know No is a book about a dog that was never taught how to live in a house with a family. He was left to live on his own and was never told "yes" or "no." When he came to live with a family, he was lost and did not know the rules. His new owner taught him the rules by teaching him "yes" and "no."

Children also need to be taught "yes and "no." Reading *Doggie Doesn't Know No* to your child helps teach this concept. In the story, Doggie's owner did not just tell him "no" and then offer a punishment. Rather, Doggie's owner showed the dog the correct behavior so he could learn to do the right thing. The same principle applies to our children. They will learn more from our showing them how to do things correctly than by punishing them for things they have done wrong.

Learning to accept "no" is difficult for children. By nature, children (and adults, too) want what they want when they want it. Yet, often parents expect their children to just accept "no" without giving any emotional response. Adults should remember that we tend to react emotionally when we are told "no." Many of us have wanted a job we did not get or failed to qualify for a home or car loan we were seeking. When things did not go our way, we were hurt.

As a parent, it is important to recognize that your child suffers emotional pain when he or she is told "no." We can choose to validate what the child is feeling by giving the child a hug and saying, "I know it hurts when you cannot have what you want. I love you." Offering these words to help heal your child's momentary emotional pain is similar to putting a band aid on a boo-boo. This validation meets the child's need.

The Power of "Yes"

Saying "no" with frequency does little to promote the connection between parent and child. Instead, it produces frustration in the parent and a feeling of hopelessness in the child. So, how do we stop being a "no-it-all" parent and begin to deepen our relationship with our children? We start simply by saying "yes" more often.

Saying "yes" to the small inconsequential requests is like "putting money in the bank." When it is time for the child to accept "no," we can more easily make a withdrawal. Further, saying "yes" more often will strengthen your relationship with the child. You will feel happier when you say "yes," and the child will feel valued and noticed.

How to Say "Yes" More Often:

Option One: Pause before you speak. Often we say "no" out of habit. If you are not ready to say "yes" to the request because you need a moment to think, you can say, "let me think."

Option Two: Consider the motive behind a possible "no" response. Are you saying "no" because you want to get your way, or because you have concerns about moral or health issues relating to the request? A child's asking to stay up late when overly tired or wanting cookies instead of veggies raises health concerns. A moral concern would arise if a five-year old child, for example, should request to watch a PG-13 movie.

We often say "no" to our children because our desire to control the situation is more important to us than saying "yes" to the request. For example, suppose your child wants to wear tennis shoes, but you want her to wear the fancy shoes that match that "oh so cute" outfit. Or suppose your child asks if you will play a game of basketball, but you are busy doing something you would rather do. If your reason for wanting to respond with a "no" is not based on moral or health concerns, say "yes" more often.

Option Three: Reverse the "no." When "no" comes flying out of your mouth and you see the disappointment in your child's face, it is ok to change your mind. You can simply say, "I'm sorry, I said 'no' without thinking."

Derived from the Trust-Based Relational Intervention® resources (Purvis & Cross, 1999-2014.)

Accepting No – Teaching Tips for Parents

By Cindy R. Lee, LCSW, LADC

If I Say 'Yes" Often, Will I Lose Control?

As a parent, you are the boss. As the boss, you have the option to share power. You decide when to say "yes" and when to say "no." If your child already comes to you with requests, this shows that the child understands that you are the boss. If the child has not yet learned your role, or if you always say "no," it is unlikely that he or she will come to you for permission. A good boss shares power as much as possible and, as a result, secures a respectful relationship with those under his supervision.   The not-so-effective boss micromanages and attempts to control every move of his subordinates. Control is not the goal. As parents, we should be striving for a balance between nurture and structure.

How Many "Yeses" Does it Take?

The more you can say "yes," the easier it becomes for your child to accept "no." The number of "yes" answers it takes to "fill up the bank" depends upon the unique needs of your child. If your child was in the foster care system or was adopted at a later age, the child will have a large deficit of "yes" answers. This is in contrast to attentive and nurturing families, where adoring parents meet their child's every need from the time the child is born. They soothe and feed their baby, change diapers, peer into those beautiful eyes and hold their child tight. These responses are all "yeses." In the earliest months of life, the child does not experience "no." The child receives nurture, love, and nourishment. Children who were denied this affectionate care in the early years need to hear "yes" more frequently.

Once your bank account is full of "yes" replies, it is time to make a withdrawal.   When a child comes to a parent with a request that is denied, the child often believes his parents *always* say "no." It sounds like this, "I never get to…. or you never let me…..or you always say 'no!'" This is where the Power of Yes Formula comes into play.

> #### The Power of Yes Formula:
> Child makes a request + Parent reminds the child of the yeses then says no = Child easily accepts no.

For example,
Child: "Mommy, may I have a cookie?"
Mom: "I said 'yes' to the doughnut this morning, and I said "yes" to the mint you ate from my purse. You have had a lot of sweets today, so this time I need you to accept 'no.'"
Child: "Ok mommy."

In order to get the "ok mommy" you BOTH HAVE TO PRACTICE! Start with this <u>fun</u> game:

> ### Three for Me Game
>
> *In a fun and playful manner, set out four small sweet treats or coins in front of the child. Have them ask for the first item with respect. For example, "Mommy, may I please have this red M&M?" You respond with "Yes you may." Repeat this for the next two items. When the child asks for the fourth item, you say "I said yes to the first candy, yes to the second candy, and yes to the third candy. This time I need you to accept no." Teach the child to respond with "ok mommy." Give the child praise for accepting no.*

The more you both practice, the easier it will be for you to say "yes" and your child to accept "no."

For more detailed information, please read *The Connected Child* by Purvis, Cross & Lyons-Sunshine.

Derived from the Trust-Based Relational Intervention® resources (Purvis & Cross, 1999-2014.)

Sweet little Doggie was left on his own.
The word "no" he was never shown.

No one told him what to do to survive.
He figured out a way to stay alive.

He stole from the trash and drank from the river.
The water was dirty and once he ate liver.

He slept where the ground was soft and warm.
He hid under the bushes when it would storm.

When he needed to potty,
he'd go by a tree.

Or in the grass where he happened to be.

Then one freezing, snowy day,
Doggie was cold and had no place to lay.

Animal Welfare pulled up.
The man had a treat.

He held it out for Doggie to eat.

Doggie was scared, but he had no option.
He was alone and soon up for adoption.

Knowing he was safe, Doggie jumped in the car.
The man drove them home. It was really far.

When they got to the house,
Doggie really had to "go."

He pottied on the rug,
and the man said, "No."

He put Doggie out and said, "Yes, Yes, Yes!
Potty out here where you won't make a mess."

Doggie was hungry. He tipped over the trash.
Food went flying! Crash! Crash! Crash!

His dad said, "No." His voice was loud.
Doggie was confused. His head was bowed.

Then his dad sweetly said, "This bowl is for you. Eating healthy food is what you should do."

Doggie wanted a nap so he jumped on the chair.
His dad said, "No" and gave him a scare.

He pulled out a pillow and said, "This is best.
Here on this bed is where you should rest."

"I like it here and really want to belong.
But everything I do seems to be wrong."

"This man is teaching me things that are new.
'No' must mean that's not what you do!"

"Accepting no is hard to do,
even though it's good for you."

"Now when daddy says 'No' to me,
I bark, 'Ok' to say I agree."

"I'm no longer all alone.
A deep love my dad has shown."

"No more 'No,' no more fear,
now 'Good job' is all I hear!"

About the Author:

Cindy R. Lee is a Licensed Clinical Social Worker and a Licensed Alcohol & Drug Counselor in private practice. Cindy is the co-founder and Executive Director of HALO Project (www.haloprojectokc.org.) Cindy lives in Edmond, Oklahoma with her husband Christopher and her children, Amanda and Jack (as well as several four-legged rescue dogs!) You can contact Cindy via email at cindy@cindyrlee.com.

More Titles:

Doggie Doesn't Know No is one of eight children's books designed to teach Trust Based Relational Intervention (TBRI) principles. TBRI is a very successful intervention designed to help foster and adopted children heal from relational trauma. TBRI was developed by Dr. Karyn Purvis and Dr. Davis Cross at the Institute of Child Development at TCU. For more information please visit www.child.tcu.edu. Other titles include:

Baby Owl Lost Her Whoo

It's Tough to be Gentle: A Dragon's Tale

The Redo Roo

The Elephant with Small Ears

84383653R00018

Made in the USA
San Bernardino, CA
07 August 2018